Famous Fables, Lasting Virtues
Tips for Parents

Now that you've read The Racers, *use these pages as a guide in teaching your child the virtues in the story. By talking about the story and engaging in the suggested activities, you can help your child develop good judgment and a strong moral character.*

About Fairness

Children have an inherent sense of fairness. In fact, most children in a group would prefer for no one to have a prize than to have prizes handed out unfairly. Most children are also bothered by injustice even if they themselves are not being treated unfairly. But fairness is not always black and white. Although the "rules" of fairness may differ according to the situation and the individuals involved, the fact that there should be a "concept" of fairness does not. Here are some ideas for getting that concept across to your child:

1. *Things aren't always equal.* Your child will undoubtedly encounter unfairness in his life—whether at school, on playdates, or at extracurricular activities. He may occasionally feel he is treated unfairly at home, especially if he has a sibling. If your child complains to you about such injustices, be sympathetic and acknowledge his frustration. Discuss any practical remedies. If there are none, gently explain that such situations sometimes occur in life, and that his unhappiness is bound to pass.

2. *Show pride in individual strengths.* In *The Racers* the Hare was the fastest, but the Snail showed determination and courage. Acknowledge the different strengths of the individuals in your family and your circle of friends. Someone may be a math whiz, while another may show great empathy. Emphasize that there are many ways to shine.

3. *Let your child help decide what's fair.* When you include your child in decision-making, he is more apt to understand the rationale and consider it fair. For example, when setting bedtimes for siblings, explain the different needs for different ages and the consequences of a lack of sleep. Ultimately, you can let them know that it's your decision, but that you are being thoughtful and even-handed in your consideration.

    With that, the Snail beamed. The perfect prize, he
thought, settling into his new mossy home. "Thank you,
thank you," he said to the judges and crowd. "I have a
great view from here and will use it well. My experience
will serve us all when I am a judge. And I vow to be
completely fair!"

    "Here, here," cried the Mule. "To total fairness." And
with that, the judges and racers all gave a cheer.

"And better than that," the Owl chimed in, "we're appointing the Snail to be one of the head judges for next year's race! After all, the Snail showed us his pluck, courage, and determination. All good qualities to judge our next contest."

Just then the Earthworm, who had overslept, arrived. "What is the first prize?" he asked.

"Entrance to the vegetable garden anytime," answered the Mule. "That was my idea. After all, the prize is going to the Hare, who needs plenty of vegetables! It makes the most sense. For second prize, we grant the Snail permission to perch on the stone wall, enjoying the moss and sunshine."

The Wild Rose kept her thoughts to herself, because that was her nature. It is too bad she did not speak them aloud. "It seems to me," she thought, "that the Sunbeam should come in first as well as second. After all, it crosses miles of space to bring us life and help us grow, and to give us our days."

So the Wild Rose stayed quiet, better to enjoy the peace of the woods and bask in the sun. She whispered only, "Thank you for making me bloom and giving me sweet perfume. Long live the Sunbeam."

"I would have voted for myself if I could have," confessed the Mule. "But as one of the judges, that would not have been fair. But the prize is not just for speed, strength, or cleverness. One can't forget beauty. Just look at the Hare's wonderful, long, perfectly-formed ears. Rather like my own! And that's why I cast my vote for the Hare!"

"Oh do hush," snapped the Butterfly. "I'm not going to make a speech. But I must tell you, the other day I hitched a ride on a train. We went whizzing right by a young hare. I'm clearly the winner. But never mind. I fly because that is who I am and what I do. A butterfly who flies … and needs no prize!" And with that, away the Butterfly flew.

Then another judge, the Fox, spoke up. "I give you my word of honor. The prizes were awarded fairly. I have judged seven times before, and have always judged the same way. I start at the beginning of the alphabet for the first-prize winner, and I start at the end for the second-prize winner. Fair is fair!"

"Since this is the eighth race, the eighth letter from the letter *A* is *H. H* stands for Hare," the Fox explained. "The eighth letter from the letter *Z* is *S* … as in Snail. Next year, first prize will go to the letter *I* and second prize to *R*. You see, I have a proper system."

The Snail, who had been quite pleased, was
growing irritated. "I really should have come in first. With
my sprained foot, I deserve nothing less. Mr. Speedy Hare
here runs fast only out of fear. He is always running away
from danger. But I'm not the type to make a fuss."

Just then, the Swallow swooped down with a squawk. "Why was I not considered as a winner? Who has been swifter than I? More graceful? Who has traveled farther? I've circled the globe!"

"Well, now, you couldn't have stated the problem more clearly," replied the Owl. "You don't settle down and stay the course. The minute it gets a bit nippy, you're gone. You have no loyalty! You're too flighty to be considered."

The Swallow persisted in making her case. "Suppose I was staying in the marsh for the winter? Then might I be considered?"

"Perhaps if you could prove it," the Owl conceded. "But we would need something official in writing from the Marsh Monitor."

"Now, now," the Owl scolded. "You came in first, so what does it matter? Anyway, there are things we consider other than speed. Determination counts. So does good will. It took the Snail nearly the entire twelve months to cross the finish line, but he sprained his foot along the way in his haste!"

"Haste!" the Hare snorted. "You call THAT haste?"

"Yes," replied the Owl. "For Snail, it was. He gave the race everything he had, and even ran with his house on his back. He showed stick-to-it-ive-ness! And for that, he deserves second place."

"First prize!" boasted the Hare. "I won it fair and square. Of course, I expected to win. After all, my friends and family are among the judges!" In fact the Hare was speedy, and he had crossed the finish line first.

Still, the Hare was not thoroughly pleased. "I don't understand," he sniffed. "It's not fair that the Snail should take second place! I find it rather insulting that he should win a place at all."

Two prizes were being offered—for first and second
place. Finally, today, the year was up! The judges and
contestants all gathered at the finish line for the awards
ceremony. Together, the judges announced that the
Hare was the first place winner. Second place was
awarded to the Snail.

The race was on! In fact, the race had been on
for an entire year. For this was not just an ordinary race,
held on a single day. This contest was being held to see
who was the fastest over a year's time.

The Racers

A Story about Fairness

Retold by Karen Baicker
Illustrated by Jon Goodell

Reader's Digest Young Families